T0197432

JIMMY
AND THE
WOLF

by:
Glenn Tewaaraton (GT) Mares

Illustrations by
Hope Mares

AuthorHouse™
1663 Liberty Drive
Bloomington, IN 47403
www.authorhouse.com
Phone: 833-262-8899

Because of the dynamic nature of the Internet, any web addresses or links contained in this book may have changed since publication and may no longer be valid. The views expressed in this work are solely those of the author and do not necessarily reflect the views of the publisher, and the publisher hereby disclaims any responsibility for them.

Any people depicted in stock imagery provided by Getty Images are models, and such images are being used for illustrative purposes only.
Certain stock imagery © Getty Images.

This book is printed on acid-free paper.

ISBN: 978-1-6655-6766-4 (sc)
ISBN: 978-1-6655-6767-1 (e)

Library of Congress Control Number: 2022914568

Print information available on the last page.

Published by AuthorHouse 08/09/2022

authorHOUSE®

JIMMY
AND THE
WOLF

This is a story about a boy named Jimmy who had a long braid. He and his father and mother lived in Colorado in the city of Denver, a remarkably busy place where people were always in such a rush to get here and there. But when summer came it was a special time for Jimmy and his parents.

Summertime for Jimmy's family meant vacation and a drive up to the Colorado Mountains for fresh air, time for relaxation and great fun. They packed up all the camping gear and food they needed and set out on the road for a wonderful journey.

The camp site was near a big lake that had fishing and swimming all day long and plenty of fresh air and open space to run and play. But there was also a deep dark forest that surrounded the campground. This forest had thousands of trees and was home for many wild animals both large and small.

The best time to catch fish is in the early morning. So together the family made plans. Jimmy and his dad would get up early and head out to the lake to fish and hopefully bring back a great catch for dinner. Jimmy's mom planned on a quiet and relaxing day and sitting down with a good book.

After they set up camp and ate a delicious meal of hotdogs and yummy roasted marshmallows, they were down for the night. Their plans were already set; Jimmy and his dad would go fishing and his mom would relax at the campsite to read one of her favorite books.

And, so it was, the morning air was cool and crisp, and the sun was rising over the mountain tops. Soon it was sunny and bright. Jimmy caught his first fish, big enough for their dinner.

"That was a great catch Jimmy!" said his father so proudly.

It happened that evening after dinner at the campsite... Jimmy caught site of a small bushy-tailed white rabbit scampering across the grass. He jumped up from the table to chase after it. Jimmy's mom yelled out to him, "Don't wonder off too far, Jimmy."

"Okay Mom," said Jimmy.

But it wasn't long before Jimmy was deep into the forest and soon realized he was lost. He didn't know what direction to go. The more he walked the deeper into the forest he went. Meanwhile back at camp Jimmy's parents had become very worried.

Of course, the little creatures and birds could not help him find his way back. Jimmy sat down on a log to discuss his troubles to a squirrel that happened to be nearby munching on an acorn. The squirrel and a few other little critters looked at Jimmy with bright, curious eyes. When suddenly, they scurried off without even a goodbye.

Jimmy was puzzled at their sudden departure, when he heard a long deep sounding growl come from behind him.

"Grrrrrr. Grrrrrr."

Slowly Jimmy turned and saw a huge ferocious looking grey wolf standing just a few feet away directly behind him. Jimmy showed no fear, not a flinch, and looked squarely into the eyes of the huge animal.

"Why do you growl at me?" asked Jimmy.

"I am hungry, and I plan to eat you," said the wolf.

"No! You will not eat me, Mr. Wolf. And I am not afraid of you," said Jimmy.

"Why aren't you afraid? I am a ferocious wolf and am very hungry."

"You will not eat me. I think a mean coyote would be a more satisfying and tasty meal for you instead of a little boy like me."

"Indeed, that is an incredibly good idea...Hmm. So be it. I would like you, a human, to be my friend. I have never had a human for a friend," said the wolf. "And by the way, my name is Oscar. What is your name?"

Jimmy's eyes brightened up and he answered, "My name is Jimmy and I would be very happy to be your friend, Oscar."

"You may live with me here in the forest forever. I will protect you from all the mean wild creatures that roam throughout. No one will ever harm you. I give you my word," said Oscar.

"Oscar," said Jimmy "I cannot live here with you forever because my home is in the city with my parents. But I can promise to return to visit you every summer. I hope you understand."

"I do understand. Your home is in the city and my home is in the forest. I cannot come to the city to visit you, but you can come to the forest to visit me. Whenever you are here we can run and jump and play. The forest is full of adventure and wonder. We will have grand times together."

"I would really like that Oscar. We will be best friends forever. That is a promise. Awesome!"

Oscar grinned and looked long and curious at Jimmy, his newfound human friend and Jimmy looked right back at Oscar with a big smile.

"Right now, Oscar, I am lost in this huge forest and I need help to find my way back to camp where my parents are surely worried by now. Please help me find my way back," said Jimmy.

"Yes, of course. Jump on my back and hold on tight."

Jimmy jumped on Oscar's back and with a good strong grip Jimmy took hold of the grey hair on the back of Oscar's neck and off they went. Jimmy and Oscar jumped over hurdles of rocks and bushes, running fast with the wind blowing at their faces. It was amazing.

While they were dashing and darting about through the forest Jimmy spotted a large bear as big as an elephant. Jimmy shouted out to Oscar, "I see a huge bear. Can we stop just for a moment to talk to him?"

Oscar said, "Oh that's Red Scruffy. He is one of my oldest friends. He would be happy to meet you. Let's go to him."

"Red Scruffy, how are you doing my friend?"

"Hello Oscar," said the bear in a very deep sounding voice. "I am very well, thank you. And who is this riding on your back?"

"Red Scruffy, I would like you to meet my human friend, Jimmy."

"I am happy to meet you Red Scruffy," said Jimmy. I would love to stay and chat with you. You are certainly a grand looking bear, but we are on a mission to find my parents. Goodbye for now."

Oscar's keen eyes spotted two coyotes out in the distance on the mountainside. The ornery looking coyotes were spying the campsite, most likely waiting for a good opportunity to pounce on Jimmy's parents. Now, by this time Oscar was very hungry and two coyotes for dinner would be a very tasty meal. The sneaky coyotes were warily moving down the mountain toward the campsite. Oscar slowed down his prance to a slow pace then halted and Jimmy jumped off.

"Jimmy, you wait here while I take care of those two coyotes that are about to attack your parents at the campsite."

It didn't take Oscar long to capture and put down the two coyotes and provide himself a good meal for later. Oscar and Jimmy were happy that Jimmy's parents were no longer the target of two wild coyotes.

Now, back safe at the campsite, Jimmy jumped off Oscar's back and ran over to his parents and gave them a big hug. Everyone was incredibly happy. Jimmy introduced Oscar to his parents. His parents were a little startled at meeting the huge wolf, but they saw that Jimmy was unafraid and quite at ease with Oscar. They invited Oscar to join them for dinner.

Oscar, however, had an enormous meal of two coyotes waiting for him up on the mountainside, so he politely declined the invitation.

"Thank you so much for the invitation to dinner, but I must return to the forest now. I hope to see all of you next summer, especially Jimmy, my new friend for life.

"And please, remember that whenever Jimmy is with me, no harm will come to him," said Oscar. "Goodbye and be safe on your trip back to the city."

This was, most definitely, an amazing summer—one that Jimmy, and Oscar would always treasure.

The End

Printed in the United States
by Baker & Taylor Publisher Services